Stephanie Dagg lives just outside Bandon, Co. Cork, with husband Chris and their three children Benjamin, Caitlín and Ruadhrí. They also have two dogs and some very spoilt chickens.

When she's not busy writing, Stephanie loves swimming and cycling, and doing arts and crafts.

Do visit Stephanie's websites at
www.booksarecool.com and
www.ecobabe.com.

Stephanie is committed to planting trees to contribute towards neutralising any carbon emisssions arising from publishing these books.

Contents

*Dedicated to everyone
who loves Christmas
as much as I do!*

MENTOR
BOOKS

This Edition first published 2005 by

MENTOR BOOKS
43 Furze Road,
Sandyford Industrial Estate,
Dublin 18.
Tel. +353 1 295 2112/3   Fax. +353 1 295 2114
e-mail: all@mentorbooks.ie

ISBN: 1-84210-330-X
A catalogue record for this book is available from the
British Library

Illustrations: Kim Shaw
Editing, Design and Layout by Mentor Books

Printed in Ireland by ColourBooks Ltd.

13 5 7 9 10 8 6 4 2

Chapter 1
Too Much Santa

Teddy Bear Jake sighed as he stood and looked at his boss, who was stretched out in an armchair in front of the fire, snoring very loudly. It was New Year's Day and Santa had been asleep since he'd arrived back at the North Pole just before dawn on Christmas Day. He didn't normally sleep this long after his busy night delivering toys to all the children.

Teddy Bear Jake was worried. Santa must be getting unfit. And there did seem to be an awful lot of him sticking out of the chair. Was he putting on weight too? That would never do. Santa must look after himself properly. He was the world's busiest man with the world's most important job, after all. It was time to do something about Santa's lifestyle.

Teddy Bear Jake tried to wake Santa up. First he tickled his nose, then he pulled his beard gently, and then he blew down his ear. But Santa only stirred slightly. Next Teddy Bear Jake tried poking him and prodding him, but Santa just snored louder. Then Teddy Bear Jake yelled 'WAKE UP' at the top of his voice. Nothing happened at all that time.

'I know what to do!' grinned Teddy Bear Jake.

He hurried off to the kitchen and came back with a huge plateful of hot, steaming mince pies. They smelled wonderful. He wafted the plate under Santa's nose a few times. Santa's nostrils began to twitch. He licked his lips sleepily. His eyelids began to flicker. Then with a loud 'Yum!', he sat up and grabbed the plate and gobbled all

Oh Santa!

the mince pies down in five seconds flat.

'Oh Santa!' said Teddy Bear Jake crossly. 'You weren't meant to do that.'

'Why ever not?' chuckled Santa. 'I'm starving! And I'd love a pot or two of tea. Could you run and put the kettle on for me please?'

'No,' replied Teddy Bear Jake grumpily. 'You can do it yourself. You need the exercise.'

'Right-ho!' smiled Santa. He tried to get up, but he couldn't move. 'Um. I appear to be stuck. I think my chair has shrunk. Can you lend me a paw here, my friend?'

But Teddy Bear Jake had to lend three paws before he was able to heave Santa out of his chair. They left a few bits of Santa's trousers behind too.

'Goodness gracious,' panted Santa. 'I'm worn out now. I think I'd better sit back down again for a rest.'

'Oh no, you don't,' protested Teddy Bear Jake, quickly pushing the chair out of the way. He couldn't face having to drag Santa out of it again. 'I think you need to go on a healthy diet. You'd better see a doctor! I'll fetch one at once!' He rushed out of the room, grabbing a paintbrush off the shelf as he went.

'That's funny,' muttered Santa. 'I didn't know there was a doctor at the North Pole. No one ever gets sick here – my special Santa magic sees to that! And I'm sure there's no need to make such a fuss. I could just cut down from six spoonfuls of sugar in my tea to five, no problem. That should do the trick nicely.'

Suddenly his boots felt tight.

'Ooh! These things hurt,' he grumbled.

He bent down to take them off but something got in the way. His tummy!

'Well, Christmas trees and tinsel!' he

exclaimed, staring at it. 'I'm sure it never used to be that big! Perhaps I do need to see a doctor.'

He limped around in his tight boots for a little while, humming Christmas carols and listening to his tummy rumble. That tiny little plateful of mince pies was hardly enough to keep a mouse alive. And where was that doctor?

Just then there was a knock at the door. In walked a Giant Panda. He had a toy stethoscope round his neck and he was wearing a white coat. He looked amazingly like an exact black and white version of Teddy Bear Jake. What's more, he smelt strongly of paint, and to top it all, he left a trail of painty footprints across the floor.

Santa shrugged. Maybe doctors always did that.

'Now then, what seems to be the trouble?' asked Doctor Panda, sitting down in Santa's chair.

'There's no trouble really,' smiled Santa. 'I'm very, very happy being plump and sleeping a lot, but my good friend Teddy Bear Jake doesn't think it's good for me.'

'And he's quite right,' replied Doctor

Panda sternly. 'Tell me, what have you eaten during the last week.'

'Nothing,' said Santa. 'I've been asleep.'

'Very well, what did you eat the week before that?'

'Let's see,' said Santa. He thought for a moment. 'Right. On Monday, Tuesday, Wednesday, Thursday, Friday and Saturday I had porridge, bacon, beans and toast for breakfast, buttered scones for tenses, elevenses and twelveses, soup and rolls for lunch, cream cakes at 3 o'clock and fish and chips for tea. Oh yes, and hot chocolate and doughnuts for supper. And again just before I went to bed. Plus a few bars of chocolate.'

The doctor tut-tutted crossly. 'And what about Sunday?'

'Well, that was Christmas Eve so I had all the usual things up to the fish and chips but then it was different. I was out working, so I had 500 million mince pies, 22 million biscuits, 47 million sausage rolls, 397 million glasses of milk and 999 thousand chocolates. Give or take a few thousand here and there.'

'What?' gasped Doctor Panda. 'All that in one night?'

'I do call on about a billion houses, you know, and the children are all so kind and leave me such nice little snacks. It would be rude not to eat them,' explained Santa.

'I don't call 500 million mince pies and all the other stuff a little snack!' spluttered the doctor.

'I use up a lot of energy, going up and down all those chimneys,' Santa protested.

'Not 500 million mince pies' worth,' frowned Doctor Panda. 'You are seriously overeating. No wonder you are so sleepy. You must stop it at once. I shall put you on my famous alphabet diet immediately.'

'I've never heard of it,' grumbled Santa. 'What's it all about then?'

'It's very simple,' smiled the doctor. 'Each week you can only eat three different sorts of foods beginning with a certain letter of the alphabet.'

Santa looked puzzled.

'Let me explain,' the doctor went on. 'The first week will be 'A' of course, so the three foods you can eat will be . . .'

'. . . apple crumble, almond pastries and apricot upside-down pudding!' grinned Santa, suddenly understanding what the doctor meant. 'I like this diet! Then for 'B' I'll have butterscotch tart, bacon butties and buns with icing and sprinkles, and 'C' will be cherry cheesecake, chocolate cookies and cheese and onion crisps!'

'No,' said the doctor firmly. 'You've got it all wrong. You can't add "crumble" or "pudding" or even "with icing and sprinkles" to anything. That's cheating. And the foods have to be healthy ones. So for your first week I'll put you down for apples, avocados and aubergines.'

'Oh,' said Santa, disappointed. 'But what about the 'B' week? Can I still have bacon?'

'You will have bananas, broccoli and beetroot,' said the doctor firmly, making a list for Santa. 'And 'C' days will be carrots, cucumber and cabbage.'

Santa pulled a face. Then he thought of something worrying.

'What happens during the 'X' week?' he asked anxiously. 'I can't think of a single food beginning with 'X'.'

'Neither can I,' agreed the doctor. 'So I guess nothing to eat that week.'

Santa went pale. 'This is a rotten diet,' he complained.

'True,' nodded Doctor Panda, smiling.

'But it works! Especially when you follow an exercise programme too.'

Santa went even paler. 'Exercise programme?' he croaked. 'As well as eating rabbit food for the next six months, I have to jump up and down and run around too?'

'Much more than that,' said the doctor happily. 'You'll be lifting weights, and jogging, and doing aerobics, and swimming, and dancing, and marching, and cycling. And that's just the first day.'

'I'm going for a lie down,' groaned Santa.

'Oh no, you're not,' answered the doctor. 'I shall send Teddy Bear Jake back in so he can get you started on the exercises as soon as possible. Now, stick to that diet, Santa! You'll love the new you. Goodbye.'

The doctor disappeared. Santa watched

him go. He felt miserable. The next twenty-six weeks were going to be ghastly. He headed off to the reindeer sheds. Stroking the reindeers' beautiful velvety noses always cheered him up.

As he walked in, Rudolph was chomping on some straw.

'That looks tastier than what I shall be eating for the next six months,' said Santa gloomily. 'I'd be much better off being a reindeer.'

And a little later Santa really wished he were a reindeer as he pounded along on the treadmill. A reindeer had four legs and loved running. Santa only had two and he hated running. He was hopeless at it.

Teddy Bear Jake was watching over him. The teddy bear was a bit damp, as if he had just come out of the shower and hadn't had time to dry himself properly. There were a few black and white splodges on his fur in different places too.

But Santa didn't notice. He was too busy puffing and panting and gasping for breath. The treadmill was horrible, like all the other exercise machines he'd just been on. Santa's elves and pixies had quickly built him a gym on Teddy Bear Jake's orders. Santa already called it 'the torture chamber'.

Teddy Bear Jake glanced at his stopwatch.

'OK, you can stop now,' he said.

'At last!' gasped Santa. He stopped running at once. But of course the treadmill kept going. Santa found himself shooting backwards along the conveyor belt. He made a grab at Teddy Bear Jake

21

but it was too late. Next second he crashed down onto the floor on his back with a mighty thud. He lay there, groaning.

'Oh Santa!' cried Teddy Bear Jake, kneeling down next to him. 'Are you OK?'

Santa managed a tiny nod. 'Why are you trying to kill me?' he croaked.

Teddy Bear Jake helped him to sit up.

'Please can't I just be fat and lazy?' Santa begged. Then he began chuckling. 'I bet I looked funny, whizzing backwards on that machine!'

Teddy Bear Jake started laughing. 'Oh Santa! If only you could have seen the look on your face! It was priceless!'

The two of them guffawed and chortled until they were exhausted. Then Santa crawled to the shower and off to bed, aching all over.

Chapter 2
Santa Gets Fit

The first few weeks went by slowly, painfully and hungrily. Santa was totally miserable. He missed his porridge and bacon and scones and cream cakes and chips and doughnuts. He missed his lovely strong, sweet cups of tea. Teddy Bear Jake only let Santa have water. And even though he put slices of lemon in it, or little ice cubes shaped like reindeers or Christmas trees to cheer Santa up, it was still just horrible, healthy, boring water. Santa missed sitting around reading too. And he especially missed pottering around the North Pole, chatting to all his elf and pixie helpers as they worked busily away. Instead Teddy Bear Jake had him exercising practically all day long and kept him strictly to the horrid diet. Santa managed to sneak off a few times and raid the fridge but Teddy Bear Jake always found out and made Santa do even more exercises to make up for being naughty!

Every day started at six o'clock. Teddy Bear Jake got Santa up and took him off for a five kilometre jog. Then it was breakfast, consisting of one of the three foods Santa was allowed that week. Next off to the gym for some weightlifting, rowing and aerobics. After that, Santa had a little rest – usually on the floor in the gym as he was too tired to go back home! Lunch followed, not that it seemed like lunch to Santa. Nibbling away at the second of his three foods wasn't any fun at all, and it certainly wasn't filling. In the afternoons Santa climbed onto the dreaded treadmill and ran and ran and ran. Then just before tea Teddy Bear Jake took him off for an hour of dancing and then a swim. And after tea, it was time for another cross-country jog and a few last stretching exercises before Santa fell exhausted and starving into bed. Once he was asleep, Teddy Bear Jake dashed off to the kitchen for a huge, secret supper!

But gradually Santa began to feel a little bit better. The running and the rowing and the weightlifting and the aerobics didn't hurt quite so much. And instead of being bright purple when he finished, he was now just a tiny bit pink. He started to enjoy swimming with the polar bears and seals amongst the ice floes, even though it was incredibly cold. And as for dancing, Santa was definitely getting into the groove!

Now that he was exercising so much, he had a lot less time to organise all the elves and pixies in the toymaking department.

He got very bothered about that, until Teddy Bear Jake persuaded him to get a mobile phone.

'You'll be able to make calls to check up on things while you're exercising,' Teddy Bear Jake told him.

'I don't know,' Santa sighed. 'These fancy phones are far too modern for me. I shall never learn how to use one properly.'

But he soon did. However, there were a few problems to start with because Santa was puffing and panting so much from all the exercise that whoever he was talking to couldn't understand a word he said! So Santa started sending texts instead. His thumbs fairly flew all over the keypad.

Easter came and went, and before long it was summer. Santa had many long, happy jogs in the night-time sunshine with Teddy Bear Jake and Rudolph. He splashed joyfully around in the sea beneath a pink and orange sky. It was really fun. And better still, Santa was up to watermelon, walnuts and watercress now. The end of the awful alphabet diet was in sight! Then finally, after a week of zucchini, zucchini and zucchini (the only food beginning with Z Teddy Bear Jake could find), it was over.

'Right,' smiled Teddy Bear Jake. 'I shall fetch the mirror. You can have a good look at the new, healthy Santa!'

Santa was nervous while he waited for Teddy Bear Jake to come back. He knew he'd lost a lot of weight because he'd been tightening his belt, hole by hole. And he could see muscles he'd never seen before appearing on his legs and arms. But what was the overall effect?

Teddy Bear Jake staggered in with a full-length mirror. He stood it up. But Santa kept his eyes closed. He couldn't bear to look!

'Come on! Take a peek!' urged Teddy Bear Jake.

Santa opened one eye, then the other. He peered cautiously into the glass.

'I say!' he smiled after a moment, looking at his reflection proudly. 'I do look rather good, don't I?'

It was true. Santa was so trim and slim – he hardly recognised himself. The only thing that was as big as ever was his white bushy beard. Santa twirled round and round in front of the mirror. But there was one hitch. His red trousers hung off him in loose folds. They looked dreadful. His jacket would, no doubt, be the same.

'I'll ask the dressmaking fairies to take your suit in,' offered Teddy Bear Jake.

'No thanks,' replied Santa. 'I fancy a change. Besides, the fur trimming makes me look fat. I want a trendier outfit.' He thought for a moment. 'How about a nice green and red stripy jumper.'

'But people say 'red and green should never be seen,' Teddy Bear Jake told him. 'You're not supposed to wear them together.'

'Tell that to a holly bush!' chuckled Santa. 'Green and red is what I shall have, please. And I'd also like a pair of janes.'

'Janes?' echoed Teddy Bear Jake, puzzled.

'Or maybe it's joans. They're trousers with a girl's name,' shrugged Santa.

Teddy Bear Jake smiled. 'I think you mean jeans. I'll go and get you some.' He rushed away and soon came back with a very fashionable pair indeed. They fitted Santa perfectly.

'Smashing!' grinned Santa.

'The fairies will have your jumper ready by teatime,' Teddy Bear Jake announced. 'Now, what about a new hat too? How about a cowboy hat? Or maybe a stripy, knitted bobble hat to go with your jumper? What do you think?'

'Oh no! I couldn't possibly part with this one,' said Santa, stroking his lovely red hat, which he never took off. 'I love it too much!'

'Oh Santa!' laughed Teddy Bear Jake.

Chapter 3
New Santa

To everyone's amazement, especially Teddy Bear Jake's, Santa kept up with his exercise programme over the following months. He was very glad indeed to give up the alphabet diet, but he cut down a lot on all the fattening, sugary food. He stayed slim and healthy – and incredibly active. He raced around the North Pole, looking sleek and smart in his stripy jumper and jeans.

One morning Teddy Bear Jake looked at the calendar.

'The first letters from children should be arriving soon, Santa,' Teddy Bear Jake said as he brought him a cup of herbal tea.

'Oh no!' groaned Santa, climbing off

the rowing machine. 'I don't have time to sit down and read all those millions of letters any more. I need to do my exercises. You must tell the children to email me or text me on their mobile phones instead. That will save me a lot of time.'

'Oh Santa!' protested Teddy Bear Jake. 'That's not fair.' He knew that a lot of children didn't have computers or mobiles. But Santa wasn't listening.

'And I can programme my phone and computer to send an instant, standard reply rather than have to write a separate answer to each letter,' Santa went on. 'That will be much more efficient and save me sitting down for hours. Oh yes, and while you're at it, please tell the children to only leave me fruit or vegetables as snacks this year, certainly nothing as fattening as mince pies or sausage rolls. Mineral water instead of milk too. Ugh!' he shuddered. 'To think of all that unhealthy food I used to scoff. What was I thinking of? Now, it's time for my ten-kilometre jog. I don't want to get lazy.'

He headed off energetically into the snow.

Teddy Bear Jake looked after him sadly. This wasn't the Santa he loved. Maybe he should have left tubby, sleepy Santa alone.

And worse was to come at the next

Christmas planning meeting. These were held on the last Friday of each month. So far this year Santa had slept through every one as he was always exhausted from all the exercises and weak from lack of food. His loud snoring and the echoing rumbling of his tummy had made it impossible for his chief helpers to get anything done at all at the meetings. So they were all delighted to see the new, healthy, lively Santa sitting at the head of the table. But not for long.

'Now then,' said Santa, starting the meeting. 'Let's have a look at what toys are hot this year. What do the children want this Christmas?'

'Electric scooters,' said a cheerful Pixie Buttercup.

'Well, they're not getting those for a start,' spluttered Santa. 'They'll make the children lazy. Give them the good old fashioned push-a-long sort instead.'

'But we've already made over a million amazing electric ones!' cried Pixie Buttercup in protest.

'You'll just have to unmake them and recycle all the parts,' said Santa firmly. 'Next?'

'Candy-floss making machines,' said Fairy Snowdrop a little timidly.

'Yuck!' shuddered Santa. 'That horrid, sticky fattening stuff. They're not having those either. They can have vegetable steamers instead. We'll get the children eating properly. I hope you're not about to tell me you've made a million of those candy-floss thingies, are you?' he asked with a frown.

'Two million actually,' whimpered the poor fairy.

Santa tut-tutted crossly. 'And what else?' he demanded

There was silence. Nobody dared tell him about the various computer and video games that were amazingly popular this year. They knew he'd disapprove of the children sitting down for hours to play them. Elf Oakwood, who was in charge of those games, quickly scribbled them out on his list and wrote 'skipping ropes' instead.

'Right. Here's what I want you all to make,' ordered Santa, and he spent the next three hours naming the various toys he approved of. By the end of the meeting, he was very pleased. This year every child was going to be getting a healthy sort of toy – whether they wanted it or not!

But Santa's helpers were dismayed. They had always thought it was their job to make all the children's dreams come true at Christmas by giving them what they'd always wanted. This year there was going to be a lot of very disappointed children.

Santa bundled out of the room to go for a long, freezing swim. Teddy Bear Jake looked round at his sad friends in the meeting room.

'Oh Santa!' he sighed.

But what could they do?

Chapter 4
Visitors

There were just three weeks to go until Christmas. Normally the whole of the North Pole was humming with activity, excitement and happiness at this time. But this year there was just the activity. Normally all Santa's helpers tingled with joy as they imagined the happy looks on the children's faces on Christmas morning as they opened their longed-for presents. But this year all they could think about was how many children would be crying with disappointment once they'd torn the wrapping paper off their parcels.

Santa was too busy exercising to notice that anything was different.

One evening there was a knock at the

door, but Santa didn't hear it. He was pounding away on his treadmill, listening to Christmas carols at full blast on his MP3. He sang along loudly, 'So here it is, Merry Christmas . . .'

The knocking went on, and on, and on . . . and on. Then it began to grow fainter and fainter. Finally it stopped. And at that moment so did Santa. He climbed off the treadmill and did some stretching exercises.

'I think I shall just pop out for a quick jog,' decided Santa. So he pulled his white mittens and scarf on and opened the door.

'Baubles and parcels!' he exclaimed. There on the doorstep were two small snowmen. 'They weren't there earlier,' thought Santa, chuckling. 'Those cheeky elves have done this!'

But suddenly one of the snowmen moved. It wiped its face with a very snowy arm. A little pink face appeared and stared up at Santa in alarm.

'Who are you?' squeaked a little boy's voice. 'You're not Santa!' He thumped the small snowman next to him. 'Sally! There's someone else in Santa's house! I reckon he must be a burglar. He's got a stripy top like burglars have!'

'Ow! No need to hit so hard, Tim!' grumbled the other snowman. It shook its head. A lot of snow fell off and revealed a little girl. She looked up at Santa too. Then she screamed.

'Ssh! Ssh!' begged Santa. 'It *is* me! I *am* Santa! Honestly!'

Sally stopped screaming and the two children glared at him suspiciously.

'You don't look like Santa,' said Tim accusingly. 'Apart from your bushy beard and your red hat.'

'Yes, you're far too thin and you've got the wrong clothes on,' agreed his sister. 'You should be fat and dressed all in red.'

'I know, children,' sighed Santa. 'It's a long story. But why are you here? And how on earth did you get here? Goodness me! Your parents must be worried sick!'

'No, it's OK, Santa, they brought us,' explained Sally. 'There they are, see!' She pointed back to two more snowmen standing by a huge heap of snow just outside Santa's gate.

'But why are you here?' gasped Santa.

'Because we don't have a computer or a mobile phone so we couldn't send you an email or a text,' explained Tim. 'We heard that we weren't allowed to write to you any more. The only way we could let you know what we wanted for Christmas was to come here ourselves and tell you.'

'Mum and Dad took time off work to bring us,' said Sally. 'They even sold the car so we could buy a sledge and some husky dogs to get here.'

'Dad has fallen down three crevices in the ice. He's covered in bruises. And Mum is so cold she hasn't been able to stop her teeth chattering for a week now,' Tim added. 'In fact, two teeth fell out last night when she gave an extra big shiver.'

'Oh dear,' sighed Santa.

'But it's worth it all just to see you, Santa,' smiled Sally. She shuffled forward and gave him a big snowy hug.

'Yes, we love you Santa.' Tim joined the hugging. 'Even if you do look funny and won't let us write you letters.'

'You'd better come in, all of you,' said Santa, feeling terrible. He waved to Tim and Sally's parents, but they didn't move.

'They're probably frozen solid again,' explained Sally. 'They've been lending us so many of their clothes to make sure we stay warm that they've been getting colder and colder every day.'

'Wait here,' ordered Santa. He dashed out into the snow and lifted up the two snowmen, one in each muscular arm. He carried the stiff, icy statues back to his house. He propped them up in front of the fire, next to Tim and Sally. Slowly they began to steam and drip. Next he ran out to the huge heap of snow and rescued the huskies.

'Right, I'd better find you something to eat,' said Santa.

He went to the kitchen and opened his fridge. But all he had were nice, slimming fruit and vegetables, like kiwis and melons, Brussels sprouts and turnips. Somehow he didn't think the frozen family would want those. They needed good warming, filling food.

He quickly phoned Gnome Piecrust the cook, and asked him to bring over four Christmas puddings, twenty hot sausage rolls, a dozen baked potatoes dripping with butter, and two gigantic jugfuls of hot chocolate with marshmallows and cream. Then he phoned Teddy Bear Jake.

'I need you right away, my friend. We have a serious problem,' he said. 'This new Santa won't do. He won't do at all.'

Chapter 5
Santa Returns

Once the frozen family were all thawed out and full to bursting with delicious food, Santa loaded them into his sleigh.

'You will remember my new electric scooter, won't you Santa, please?' Tim reminded him. 'That way I'll be able to scoot around with the other kids down my street, even though I've got a wonky leg.'

'And my candy-floss maker,' begged Sally. 'Then I'll be able to give some fab parties and make some new friends. I don't really have any at the moment, you see.'

Santa nodded thoughtfully. A pushalong scooter and a vegetable steamer wouldn't be any good for these two children. And no doubt many of the other children who had asked for the same things as Tim and Sally had very good reasons for wanting them too. They weren't just being lazy or greedy. Santa felt very guilty indeed. How could he have been so mean? He was never like this in the old days.

Then Rudolph the Reindeer took off to take the family safely home. Santa and Teddy Bear Jake waved goodbye until the sleigh was out of sight.

'Come along, Teddy Bear Jake,' sighed Santa. 'We've got rather a lot to do between now and Christmas. We've got to make toys that children really want. We've got to make Christmas magic again. We've got to make dreams come true. We must let the children know that of course they can write to me – as many letters as they like. I'll reply to each and every one, just like I always used to.'

'So where shall we start?' asked Teddy Bear Jake. He was delighted at the news but overwhelmed by all the hard work ahead. Christmas was nearly here.

Santa chuckled. 'We start with food! I've got to fit into my old suit again. The children don't want a super skinny, spoilsport Santa in a stripy jumper. They want cuddly, kind Santa all in red. Please fetch me as much food as you can carry. Take a wheelbarrow with you. No, take two! Santa's back! I thought I might start with some porridge, bacon, beans and toast, followed by scones and soup and rolls, then a few cream cakes and an extra large portion of fish and chips. Don't forget doughnuts and a couple of platefuls of mince pies. And no herbal tea! '

'Oh Santa!' laughed Teddy Bear Jake. 'Thank goodness for that!'

MORE BOOKS FROM THE *OH!* SERIES

NEW — Oh Auntie! — Stephanie Dagg

Robyn and Paul have a special babysitter for the weekend – Auntie! However, farm life causes problems for a lady used to living in the city.

Oh Teacher! — Stephanie Dagg

Oh Baby! — Stephanie Dagg

Oh Grandad! — Stephanie Dagg

Oh Gran! — Stephanie Dagg

Oh Dad! — Stephanie Dagg